D1137404

This book
belongs to

....

A Willow Tree Wood Adventure

Little Fox and the Fairy

A Willow Tree Wood Adventure

Little Fox and the Fairy

J. S. Betts

Willow
Tree

A CIP catalogue record for this book is
available from the British Library

This edition published by Willow Tree Books, 2019
Willow Tree Books, Tide Mill Way, Woodbridge, Suffolk, IP12 1AP

0 2 4 6 8 9 7 5 3 1

Willow Tree Books and associated logos are trademarks and/or
registered trademarks of Imagine That Group Ltd

ISBN: 978-1-78958-182-9
Printed and bound in Great Britain
by Bell and Bain Ltd, Glasgow

www.willowtreebooks.net

For Wren
Love Daddy x

Contents

Chapter One
A Snowy Discovery

"Perfect!" said Molly, as she rummaged through the box where Grandma kept her bits and bobs. "We can use these for our den!" She passed her brother Tom a big ball of green gardening string and two thick woollen blankets. Grandma had already given them a waterproof canvas that she didn't want any more. Now they had everything they needed!

It was the week after Christmas and Molly and Tom were staying at Grandma's cottage in Willow Tree Wood. They were building a den in the living room while Grandma was busy in the kitchen. They had already pushed two sofas together and now they tied the canvas over the top to give their den a roof.

"I learnt this knot in Brownies," explained Molly, as she tied strings to the eyelets on each corner of the canvas.

"We can use those cushions to block up this end," suggested Tom, excitedly. "Then our den will be really cosy!"

Finally, Molly placed the two woollen

blankets on the floor of the den. Then she and Tom crawled inside. There was plenty of room for both of them. It was perfect!

"That looked like hard work," said Grandma, bending down to peer inside the

snug den. "I expect you two will need a break! I've made you some hot chocolate and biscuits."

In their cosy den, Molly took a sip of her drink. She had never tasted such lovely hot chocolate before. It tasted somehow ... magical.

"I love staying at Grandma's," Molly whispered to Tom.

"And I love biscuits!" laughed Tom, reaching for another one.

"Molly! Tom!" called Grandma. "Come and look out of the window."

Tom scrambled out of the den and reached the window before Molly had even put her hot chocolate down.

"Snow!" Tom gasped, pressing his nose

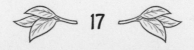

against the glass. Molly ran to join her
brother and peered outside. He was right
– it was snowing! Big, fat snowflakes fell
as slowly as feathers and filled the air with
magic. Even though Molly and Tom were
dressed in warm winter jumpers, the sight
of snow made Molly shiver.

"If it snows all night," said Molly, "then
tomorrow is going to be brilliant!"

When Molly woke the next morning,
the little bedroom was strangely quiet.
She jumped out of bed and rushed to open
the curtains – Willow Tree Wood looked

like another world! Everything lay under a thick white blanket of snow. Molly felt the excitement rise up in her chest like the bubbles in a fizzy drink.

After a quick breakfast, Molly and Tom put on their hats, scarves, gloves and boots, and ran outside. "I'm going to make a snowman," called Molly, starting to roll a

ball of snow around the garden.

"I'm making a snow angel," laughed Tom, lying on his back and moving his arms and legs up and down to make an angel shape in the snow.

When Molly finally stopped to admire her snowman's big, round body she heard something strange – a faint squeaking

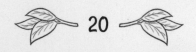

noise, like a rusty door opening and closing.

"Can you hear that?" Molly asked her brother. Tom stopped what he was doing and listened. He nodded, his eyes wide open and his cheeks glowing red from the cold.

Molly and Tom followed the noise until they came to an old shed where Grandma kept the wood for the fire. In the furthest corner of the shed sat a little fox cub. He was scruffy and damp, as if he'd fallen in water. Molly thought he looked very sorry for himself.

"Perhaps he's lost," she whispered. "Let's go and tell Grandma."

Grandma listened carefully as Molly

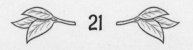

and Tom told her what they had seen. She thought for a minute. "I have just the thing," she said, opening the kitchen cupboard and taking out a tin of cat food. She put the food in a bowl, filled another bowl with water and handed them to Molly and Tom.

The children tiptoed back to the shed, put the bowls just inside the door, and then left the fox cub alone, just as Grandma said they should.

Later that day, Molly and Tom checked the shed again. Although the door was open, the little fox cub was still there. Molly thought he looked even sadder than before. "I'm worried, Tom," she whispered.

Back inside the house, Molly explained

her worry to Grandma. "I think he's cold," she said. "Maybe the snow is too deep for him to get home!"

"Can we keep him, Grandma?" asked Tom, crossing his fingers hopefully.

"You can't keep him," Grandma answered kindly. "A fox is a wild animal, not a pet. He belongs out there, in the woods. But we can look after him until the snow melts. You two wait here."

Grandma found an old cat box and went out to the shed. Soon she had brought the little fox cub inside. She placed the box down carefully in a warm corner of the living room. Bobby the dog and Whiskers the cat came to have a look, but neither of them seemed very interested.

"Let's call him Winter," suggested Molly.

"That's a great idea," agreed Grandma.

As Molly fell asleep that night, she couldn't stop worrying about the little fox cub. Would Winter ever find his way home?

Chapter Two
Fox Watch

That night, more snow fell on Willow Tree Wood. The next morning, Winter was curled up snugly in the cat box, his bushy tail laid over his nose like a blanket.

"I think Winter slept well!" chuckled Grandma, passing Tom a bowl of cat food for the little fox cub. "Let's give him some

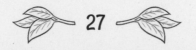

breakfast, shall we?"

Molly opened the cat box door so Tom could put the bowl inside, then she shut it again carefully. The little fox cub stood up and shook himself, then gulped down the food eagerly.

"He must have been hungry!" said Tom quietly.

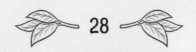

Molly was pleased to see that Winter looked a lot happier, and a lot fluffier, than the day before. She looked at the cub closely. His fur was a lovely deep red colour, with a large white patch that stretched from his chest up to his chin. His paws looked as if they were dipped in black, and the very end of his tail was as white as snow. Molly and Tom watched as Winter finished eating, then started licking his paws.

"Do you think he's ready to go home now, Grandma?" asked Tom.

"I think so, Tom," said Grandma. "We should let him go back to the woods as soon as possible."

Molly knelt down beside the cat box.

Winter's brown eyes were opened wide, and his ears pricked up as he gazed back at her. Molly thought he looked as if he understood exactly what they were saying.

Grandma carried the cat box out into the garden. She set it down gently on the path that led out of the gate and into Willow Tree Wood.

"Ready, Winter?" said Molly, before carefully opening the door. The little fox cub took a few cautious steps out of the box, before trotting off towards the trees. Just before the path dipped down and disappeared, Winter turned and looked back at them, before bounding out of sight.

"That," gasped Tom, "was awesome!"

"I hope he finds his way home," said

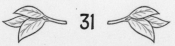

Molly, looking out into the woods.

Breakfast was Molly's favourite –
thick stacks of fluffy blueberry pancakes
covered in warm maple syrup, and more
of Grandma's special hot chocolate. After
they had helped to clear up, Molly and
Tom decided to go for a walk in the woods.
Snow clung to the dark tree trunks and
piled in small drifts here and there.

"My face is cold, but my tummy is nice
and warm," said Tom, grinning. "Grandma
makes the best breakfasts!"

Molly was about to agree, when a red

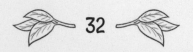

shape appeared on the path ahead of them.

"Is that Winter?" asked Tom, stopping in his tracks.

"I think so," whispered Molly. "Keep quiet. We don't want to scare him."

"I don't think he looks scared at all," replied Tom.

Tom was right – Winter didn't look scared. In fact, he looked pleased to see them! The little fox cub took two steps towards them, then turned and walked away up the path, his white-tipped tail waving in the air like a flag. Molly and Tom watched in amazement as Winter stopped and yelped in their direction.

"Maybe he wants us to follow him," said Molly. "Okay, Winter," she called, "lead the way and we'll follow you."

Winter set off at a trot, leading Molly and Tom along a winding path to a bridge that crossed a little stream. The fox cub bounded off the path and followed the stream up the hill until the water disappeared underground.

"This must be the source of the stream," said Molly, pointing at the spring that bubbled out of the ground. The children watched as Winter trotted over to a huge oak tree that stood in a clearing. Freshly dug earth was scattered around, and there was a hole beneath the tree's roots. Winter paused for a second, sprang happily into the air, and then disappeared down the hole.

"That must be where Winter lives!" cried Molly. "I think he wanted to show us he got home safely."

Tom was already inspecting the oak tree. "Wow," he said, as he disappeared behind its massive trunk. "I bet this is the biggest tree in Willow Tree Wood!"

When Tom didn't reappear Molly began to wonder where he'd gone. At last she heard his excited voice from the other side of the tree.

"Molly, quick!" he called. "You'll never believe what I've found!"

Chapter Three
Fairy Magic

Tom was staring, open-mouthed, at a
large root that stuck out from the tree
like a bent knee. Molly looked closer and
saw tiny little steps cut into the root. The
steps wound up from the ground until they
reached a tiny wooden door with a golden
knocker. Above the door were three little

windows that glowed with a warm light.

"It's a tiny house ... a fairy house!" said
Tom.

"It looks so real!" whispered Molly, her
eyes wide with astonishment. She knelt
down so she could peer through the largest
window. "Wow!" she gasped.

Inside, Molly could see a beautiful
room. In the middle of the room was a tiny
wooden table with eight tiny chairs around
it. She peered closer. On the table was a
cake stand full of teeny-tiny cupcakes, and
at the back of the room was a fireplace,
where a fire no bigger than a pebble was
glowing red and orange. Molly had never
seen anything so wonderful.

"There's a bedroom in here!" said Tom,

who was kneeling down to look in one of the other windows. "There's a bed, a cupboard, even pictures on the walls! And they're all tiny! You don't think it's real do you, Molly?" asked Tom. "You don't think Willow Tree Wood is actually ..."

"Magical?" finished Molly. The two children looked at each other in amazement.

Curiously, Molly pushed at the front door with one finger. It swung open easily and there, standing with her arms crossed angrily, was a fairy! She was no taller than the finger Molly had used to open the door.

"Excuse me!" exclaimed the fairy, her sparkly wings buzzing crossly. "Haven't you heard of knocking?"

Molly opened her mouth, but she was so shocked that she couldn't even speak.

"Are you … real?" asked Tom. "I've never met a fairy before. You're so small!"

"I'm not small," replied the fairy grumpily. "You're big! And I've never met a

human before. There aren't any in Willow Tree Wood. I heard that humans are dangerous."

"We're just children," explained Molly. "We're not dangerous at all. My name's Molly, and this is my brother, Tom. What's your name?"

"My name's Sparkle," replied the fairy uncrossing her arms and smiling for the first time.

"That name suits you," said Molly, admiring the fairy's sparkly wings. "I love your house, Sparkle. It looks so lovely and cosy!"

"Actually, it isn't that cosy any more," answered Sparkle. "This tree is so old that it's starting to get holes and cracks in it.

Little Fox and the Fairy

There's a hole in that branch up there that lets the rain in. And now there's a crack in the back of the tree where the wind blows through!"

Molly and Tom glanced at each other and nodded. They both knew just what the other was thinking.

"We can help!" they said at exactly the same time.

Chapter Four
A Clever Plan

Molly and Tom ran all the way; past the bubbling spring, alongside the tumbling stream, then along the winding path through the trees until they were back at Grandma's.

Grandma was sitting in her favourite chair, knitting a scarf. Bobby the dog was

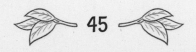

sleeping by her feet and Whiskers the cat was curled up by the fire.

"What are you two up to?" asked Grandma, her eyes twinkling.

"You won't believe ..." started Tom.

"Nothing!" interrupted Molly. "Well, we're making another den," she said. "Can we take the waterproof canvas and string?"

"Of course," said Grandma. "Just make sure you stay warm out there. It's cold outside!"

"It's probably best we don't tell Grandma about the fairy house," explained Molly, as they rushed back into the woods. "I'm not sure she'd understand." Tom nodded in agreement, although he thought

that if anyone could understand it would be Grandma.

Back at the fairy tree, Molly made sure that this time she knocked carefully at the door with a single fingernail. When Sparkle opened the door, the children showed her the canvas and string excitedly.

"We've got a plan to make your house as good as new!" announced Molly, before explaining their idea to the little fairy. Sparkle was so pleased that she flew into the air, her wings spreading fizzing bursts of rainbow colours that drifted back down to the ground.

Molly got straight to work and tied string to each corner of the canvas. Then

Sparkle took the ends of two of the strings and flew them up and over the branch, so they dangled back down on the other side. Molly and Tom took hold of one string each and hoisted the canvas over the branch until it completely covered the hole. Then, with Sparkle's help, they tied the strings tightly in place.

"That should stop the rain from getting in!" said Molly, feeling pleased with their work.

Next, they had a look at the big crack in the back of the tree.

"I know what to do," said Tom. "First we need some stones."

"There are lots of stones by the stream," suggested Molly.

"Good idea!" said Tom, and they ran back to the stream to gather as many big, flat stones as they could carry.

Tom stacked the stones in a pile in front of the hole, then Molly helped to pack earth around the stones to make a wall. It was cold and dirty work, and Molly was glad when they had finished and washed their hands in the icy spring water.

"Thank you so much!" said Sparkle. "Our house will be cosy again now!" The little fairy disappeared inside the house before returning with two acorn cups.

"You must be thirsty," she said, passing one cup to Molly and the other to Tom.

Molly tilted her head back and held the

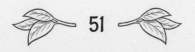

tiny cup to her mouth, turning it upside

down. Three or four drops of liquid fell on

to her tongue. "That's delicious!" she said.

"Yummy," agreed Tom, licking his lips

and grinning. "What drink is this? It tastes

sort of … colourful."

"It's rainbow dew," explained Sparkle, happily. "We fairies collect it from the ends of rainbows. I'm glad you like it."

Sparkle had left the front door of her house ajar and Tom bent down to peek inside. "I wish we were small so we could see inside your house," he said.

All at once, there was a great noisy *whoooosh* and everything around Molly and Tom seemed to grow … and grow … and grow!

Chapter Five
A Wish Come True

Molly looked at Tom and then down at herself. Everything hadn't grown – they had shrunk! The children were now about the same size as Sparkle!

"Wh ... what happened?" asked Tom, staring around in wonder.

"You wished to be small," replied

Sparkle, "and I granted your wish. Now you can come into our house and look around!"

Molly and Tom followed Sparkle up the steps in the tree root and through the door with the golden knocker. Everything that had looked so tiny before now seemed a normal size. The table ... the chairs ... even the cupcakes on the cake stand!

"We'd better not stay too long," Molly said to Tom, "or Grandma will be worried."

"It'll be fine," said Sparkle. "A fairy hour is only a human minute. You can explore as long as you like. But first let's have a cupcake and some hot chocolate!"

Sparkle showed Molly and Tom to two comfy armchairs. Tom pointed at a big log

Little Fox and the Fairy

that was crackling on the fire.

"That log," he whispered, his eyes shining, "is really only the size of a matchstick!"

Sparkle appeared with three mugs of hot chocolate, and then they each chose a cupcake from the cake stand. Sparkle's was white with multicoloured sprinkles, Tom's was covered in a thick layer of shiny chocolate, and Molly's was decorated with swirls of red and white icing. Molly bit into her cupcake, and a lovely gooey filling spilled out. It tasted of summer berries and was the most delicious thing she had ever eaten!

Tom enjoyed his cupcake too, and his face was soon smudged with chocolate. "This is yummy," he mumbled happily.

Next, Molly took a sip of the hot chocolate. "This tastes like Grandma's hot chocolate!" she said in surprise.

"It can't be the same as your Grandma's," replied Sparkle. "It's a special recipe that only fairies know. It brings magic to everything."

Once they had finished their hot chocolate and cake, Sparkle suggested that Molly and Tom set off to explore the house. It was much bigger than it looked

Little Fox and the Fairy

from the outside. There were long, curving corridors, and spiral staircases that wound round and round. Each room they looked in was full of amazing things. In some rooms there were tiny wooden chests full of delicate flower petals or colourful, shimmering stones. In others there were wardrobes hanging with twinkly tops, wispy skirts, and dainty dresses in pinks, purples, greens and browns. There were tiny bathrooms with sinks and baths

made from shiny seashells. And there were pretty bedrooms with beds made from the softest moss, and delicate silk curtains at the windows.

At last, Molly and Tom arrived back in the room where they had started. But there was no sign of their new friend.

"Perhaps Sparkle is outside," suggested Molly, opening the front door. "Let's see if we can find her."

Chapter Six
Woodland Dash

"Sparkle!" called Molly. "Where are you?"

Outside, the snowy clearing was quiet, and Molly and Tom's new friend was nowhere to be seen. Molly looked around. *Where did that fairy go?* she thought.

"So you're looking for Sparkle too, are you?" asked a grumpy voice. Molly and

Tom turned around, startled. A cross-looking fairy squinted down at them. She was sitting on a white mouse fitted with stirrups, reins and a saddle, just like a tiny horse!

"Sparkle is always late," sighed the

fairy, "especially when it's time for exercising the mice." There was a squeak as a brown mouse appeared from behind the white one.

"I'm Ivy, and as Sparkle's not here, perhaps you two can help me instead," suggested the fairy. "Jump on!"

"On ... that brown mouse?" asked Molly, uncertainly.

"Of course! Fluffy is trained," huffed Ivy. Molly and Tom looked at each other and shrugged. Molly pulled herself up into the saddle, then helped her brother up behind her.

"Giddy-up!" called Ivy, and her white mouse started off over the snow.

"How do I steer ...?" called Molly.

But before she could finish, they were
speeding after the white mouse.

"You don't need to steer," laughed Ivy.
"You just need to hold on!"

Molly grabbed hold of the reins, and
Tom grabbed hold of Molly. Ivy was right,
Molly didn't need to steer at all. It was
more like riding a rollercoaster
than a horse!

The two mice scurried through a gap under a thick green bush, then rushed over the snow, before leaping on to a fallen tree trunk. The trunk rose upwards, and they climbed higher and higher above the woodland floor.

Molly glanced down to her side and gulped.

At fairy size, it was a long way down to the snow below! Molly concentrated on holding the reins tight and watching the white mouse in front of them. She could hear Fluffy breathing and feel the soft mouse fur beneath her hands. She was just starting to enjoy the ride, when all of a sudden, the white mouse disappeared!

Molly peered ahead. They were coming to the end of the tree trunk! But, instead of stopping, Fluffy sped forward even faster … and then jumped into space!

"Arrgghh!" yelled Molly.

"Woo-hooh!" shouted Tom.

Whump! Fluffy landed in a deep snowdrift with Molly and Tom still sitting safely on her back. The mouse squeaked

happily, shook herself and set off again.
They soon caught up with Ivy's white
mouse and Molly's heart thumped in her
chest as they dashed in and out of bushes
and around trees. Finally, they darted
through a hollow log before arriving back

at the fairy house.

"That was brilliant!" panted Tom, as first he then Molly slid off Fluffy's back on to the snow. Fluffy squeaked twice. Her panting blew clouds of steam into the cold air.

"Thank you," said Ivy, looking much happier now. "You did very well. You can come back and help next week if you like."

"Yes, please!" said Tom.

"Um, maybe," fibbed Molly, who had no intention of riding a mouse again, ever!

Ivy rode her mouse off into the woods, leading Fluffy behind her. Molly caught her breath while Tom wandered off to explore. A dripping noise filled the clearing as sunlight started to melt the snow in the branches.

"Look at this!" shouted Tom. Molly made her way over to where her brother was standing. A drop of water as big as Tom's head hung from a blade of grass in front of him. Tom was staring at it and giggling.

"What's so funny?" asked Molly curiously.

"I look all ... stretched!" laughed Tom. Molly could see what he meant; the water drop was like one of those funny mirrors at fairgrounds! As she moved her head, her reflection changed shape – first longer and thinner, then wider and fatter.

"That's so weird!" laughed Molly, putting an arm around her brother so they could both look into the mirror at once.

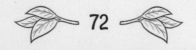

As they pulled funny faces, Molly noticed a brown blob appear above their heads in the water droplet. The blob grew larger and larger. Suddenly, Molly threw herself and Tom to the snowy ground – a moment before a blur of brown flew right over their heads!

A weasel! Molly knew about weasels.

They were small, fast hunters. Except this one wasn't small at all – it was as big as they were! They were in danger!

"Quick!" shouted Molly, dragging Tom to his feet. "We need to get back to Sparkle's house." Molly grabbed her brother's hand and they ran as fast as they could back towards the fairy tree, but the weasel was quicker – their way was blocked! The children turned and ran behind a small tree, then ducked down behind a fallen branch that lay in the snow.

"Are we safe now?" whispered Tom.

"I hope so," Molly whispered, then put her finger to her lips. "Shhh!"

Chapter Seven
Winter to the Rescue

Molly and Tom tucked themselves in close to the fallen branch. They hugged their knees up to their chests to make themselves as small as they could, and Molly pulled a big leaf down in front of them. She tried to breathe as quietly as possible, but there was nothing she could

do to make her heart beat more quietly.
It sounded as loud as a drum!

Molly heard a cracking noise of a paw
step on a dry leaf. Then again, and again.
Crack ... crack ... crack! *It must be getting
closer*, she thought.

"Get ready to run!" she mouthed to
Tom, who nodded in agreement.

But it was too late! Molly and Tom froze
as the weasel stepped around the edge of
the fallen branch. Its eyes narrowed and it
bent down, ready to pounce.

Suddenly, there was a flash of red and
something landed in front of them. Tom
gasped and Molly grabbed his hand. Was it
another weasel? No! It was ...

"Winter!" cried Tom. It was definitely

the little fox cub, with his white-tipped tail and his four dark socks. Winter stood in front of them, facing the weasel. His red fur was puffed out to make him look as big as possible, and he growled menacingly.

The weasel looked at Winter, then at the children, and then back at Winter again. Then it showed its teeth before turning and running off into the trees.

"Winter, you saved us!" said Molly gratefully. Now they were fairy-sized, Winter no longer looked like such a little cub. He was bigger than they were!

Winter turned around to face them and lay down near them in the snow. The fox cub was as friendly as ever and obviously happy to see them. Molly and Tom reached

out to gently stroke his neck and head.
Molly thought that Winter's red fur looked
more beautiful than ever. And now she
was fairy-sized his fur was so thick that
her arm almost disappeared into it as she
stroked his neck.

Winter wasn't growling any more. He was making a contented rumbling noise.

"I think he likes being stroked!" said Tom, scratching Winter behind the ear, the way Grandma's dog Bobby liked to be scratched.

"Thank you, Winter," said Molly, looking into the fox cub's beautiful brown eyes. "You're a really great friend!"

Winter tilted his head to one side and pricked his ears up, listening to Molly. Then he stood up, yelped happily, and trotted off into the trees with his tail waving behind him.

Chapter Eight
Forever Friends

Safely back in Sparkle's house again, Molly and Tom shut the door behind them.

"Phew," said Tom. "Thank goodness for Winter!"

"I know!" agreed Molly, sitting down in one of the chairs in front of the crackling fire. "Being fairy-sized is fun ... but

dangerous! And how will we ever get back to Grandma's now we're so small? It'll take us ages!"

Molly and Tom were both quiet for a minute. Maybe this hadn't been such a good adventure after all, thought Molly.

"I know what to do," said Tom, suddenly. "I'll just wish to be big again! I wish we were ..."

"Wait!" interrupted Molly. "We'd better go outside first! We wouldn't even fit in this house at our normal size!"

When they were back at the bottom of the steps outside Sparkle's house, Tom looked at his sister. "I hope Sparkle can hear me," he said, crossing his fingers and closing his eyes. "I wish we were back to our normal size again!"

Once again there was a great noisy *whoooosh*, but this time everything around Molly and Tom seemed to shrink ... and shrink ... and shrink!

When the whooshing stopped, Molly looked around and was relieved to see that they were back to their normal size again. "Well done, Tom!" she said, giving her normal-sized little brother a great big hug.

Suddenly, there was a buzz and a flurry of glitter around their heads as Sparkle appeared, as if from nowhere.

"I was just checking on my squirrel friends," explained the fairy, "but I hurried back to see you when I heard Tom wishing."

"Hello, Sparkle!"

cried Molly, happy to see their new fairy friend.

"We've had the most amazing time ..." said Tom.

"... And we've loved getting to know you," added Molly, "but it's time for us to go back to Grandma's."

"I understand," said Sparkle, smiling. "Thank you so much for fixing my house. Now us fairies will be cosy for the rest of winter."

"We'll come back to visit you again!" called Molly and Tom together as they waved goodbye.

Then the children ran all the way home – past the bubbling spring, alongside the tumbling stream, then along the

winding path through the trees until they finally arrived back at Grandma's. Grandma, Bobby and Whiskers were all exactly where they had left them. It was as if none of the adventure had really happened at all!

That night, Molly and Tom gave Grandma a goodnight hug before they went up the stairs to bed. Mum was coming to collect them the next morning.

"Have you had a good holiday?" asked Grandma. "I was worried you would find it boring here."

"Boring?" laughed Molly, "No way! It's been the best holiday ever!"

"Can we come back to stay with you in Willow Tree Wood again, Grandma?" asked

Tom hopefully.

"Of course you can. Willow Tree Wood is a magical place. You can visit whenever you like!"

Upstairs in the cosy bedroom, Molly and Tom jumped into their beds and pulled up the covers. Molly's brain was whirring with all the things they had seen and done ... Winter, Sparkle, the fairy house, cupcakes, hot chocolate, the weasel ...

"Goodnight, Molly," yawned Tom. "Sleep well."

"Goodnight, Tom," replied Molly,

before turning off her bedside lamp.

Somewhere in the darkness outside an owl hooted. Molly was just about to close her eyes when she thought she saw a faint sparkle of light outside the window.

"Did you see that?" she asked.

But Tom was already fast asleep.

If you enjoyed this book, join Molly and her brother Tom for another magical Willow Tree Wood adventure.

In Little Deer and the Dragon, Molly and Tom discover a baby deer left all on its own. With the help of a forgetful wizard called Wilbur, a small dragon and a special wish, will the Willow Tree Wood magic be strong enough to save the day?

A Willow Tree Wood Adventure

Little Deer and the Dragon

J. S. Betts

Magic is just around the corner!

ISBN: 978-1-78958-319-9

If this is your book, you
can fill in these pages yourself.
If you have borrowed it, or it belongs
to a library, write and draw your
answers on some clean paper.

Date I started this book   ....

Date I finished this book   ....

The story is about

....

....

....

....

The bit I like best is

....

....

....

....

Can you remember all of
the characters? Write a list here.

....

....

....

....

....

....

....

....

My favourite character is

....

I like them because

....

....

....

....

What does Tom make in the snow?

....

Where do Molly and Tom find Winter?

....

What do Molly and Tom give Winter to eat?

....

What drink does Grandma make
for Molly and Tom?

....

What pets does Grandma have?

....

What colour are Winter's paws?

....

What do Molly and Tom eat
at Sparkle's house?

....

Winter saves Molly and Tom from a
woodland creature. What is it?

....

If you had a magical wish,
what would it be?

....

....

Draw your wish here.

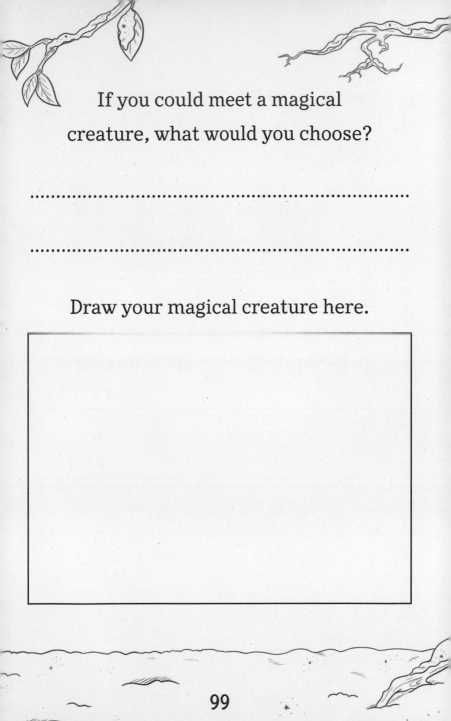

If you could meet a magical
creature, what would you choose?

....

....

Draw your magical creature here.

I give this book .... marks out of 10.

The friend I would
lend this book to is

....

Three words that describe this book

....

....

....

Recommend this book
in your own words.

You should read this because

....

....

....

....

....

....

....

Design your own book cover for
Little Fox and the Fairy here.